P9-BYK-712

DATE DUE

FOX AT SCHOOL

by Edward Marshall
pictures by James Marshall

PUFFIN BOOKS

For Jocelyn and Matthew Hayes

PUFFIN BOOKS
Published by the Penguin Group
Penguin Books USA Inc., 375 Hudson Street, New York, New York 10014, U.S.A.
Penguin Books Ltd, 27 Wrights Lane, London W8 5TZ, England
Penguin Books Australia Ltd, Ringwood, Victoria, Australia
Penguin Books Canada Ltd, 10 Alcorn Avenue, Toronto, Ontario, Canada M4V 3B2
Penguin Books (N.Z.) Ltd, 182–190 Wairau Road, Auckland 10, New Zealand

Penguin Books Ltd, Registered Offices: Harmondsworth, Middlesex, England

First published in the United States of America by Dial Books for Young Readers, 1983
Published in a Puffin Easy-to-Read edition, 1993

1 3 5 7 9 10 8 6 4 2

LIBRARY OF CONGRESS CATALOGING-IN-PUBLICATION DATA
Marshall, Edward.
Fox at school / by Edward Marshall;
pictures by James Marshall.   p.   cm.—(Puffin easy-to-read)
"Reading level 2.0"—T.p. verso.
"First published in the United States of America by Dial Books
for Young Readers, a division of Penguin Books USA Inc., 1983"—T.p. verso.
Contents: Fox on stage—Fox escapes—Fox in charge.
ISBN 0-14-036544-3
[1. Foxes—Fiction. 2. Schools—Fiction.]
I. Marshall, James, 1942– ill. II. Title. III. Series.
[PZ7.M35655Fog 1993]
[E]—dc20   93-2721   CIP   AC

Puffin® and Easy-to-Read® are registered trademarks of Penguin Books USA Inc.
Printed in the United States of America

Reading Level 2.0

FOX
ON
STAGE

4

Fox wanted a part
in the class play.
"We must be fair,"
said Miss Moon.
And she put everyone's name
into a shoe box.
"Let's see who will play
the pretty princess,"
said Miss Moon.
She drew out
the first name.

"The pretty princess
will be played by Carmen,"
said Miss Moon.

"Oh, goody!" said Carmen.
"And now for the part
of the mean dragon," said Miss Moon.
Fox held his breath.

"The mean dragon
will be played by Junior,"
said Miss Moon.

"I'll do my best," said Junior.
"And now for the part of the
handsome prince," said Miss Moon.
Fox bit his nails.

"That part goes to Fox,"
said Miss Moon.

"Hot dog!" said Fox.

"Rats," said Dexter.

"Everyone else will play
flowers and trees," said Miss Moon.

"Gosh," said Fox.

"The handsome prince!"

"Now, now," said Miss Moon.

"It is a hard part.

You must learn it by heart."

"Don't worry," said Fox.

9

That night Fox could not sleep.

He was thinking about the play.

"I'll be great!" he said.

"The girls will follow me around!"

"Fox is acting funny," said Louise
the next morning.
"So I see," said Mom.
"You may bow," said Fox.

"Do you know your part?" said Louise.
"There's nothing to it," said Fox.

At recess Junior and Carmen
worked on their parts.
"Come on, Fox," they said.
But Fox was busy.

"I will be a big hit,"
he told the girls.

The next day at play practice
Carmen and Junior
were very nervous.
"I may throw up,"
said Carmen.
"Calm down," said Fox.
"Is everybody ready?"
said Miss Moon.
"Curtain going up!"

"Here I am, all alone in the forest,"
said the pretty princess.

"Ah-ha!" cried the mean dragon.

"I am going to eat you up!"

"Help! Help! Who will save me?"
cried the pretty princess.

Everyone looked at Fox.

But Fox just stood there.

"*Who* will save me?"

cried the pretty princess again.

And everyone looked at Fox.

"Uh," said Fox.

Miss Moon was very cross.

"*You* did not study your part!"

she said to Fox.

"You are not serious

about this play."

"Miss Moon, Miss Moon," said Dexter.
"I know the part of
the handsome prince.
And I know it by heart!"
"Really, Dexter?" said Miss Moon.

The night of the play
everyone was excited.

"I hope I don't throw up,"
said Carmen.

"I hope I don't forget my lines,"
said Junior.

But no one forgot.

Carmen was very pretty
as the princess.

Junior made a fine dragon.

Dexter was very good
as the handsome prince.

And Fox...

"You were the best tree
in the whole play," said Louise.

"Just wait until *next* year,"
said Fox.

FOX
ESCAPES

DING! DING! DING!

"Fire drill!" cried Dexter.

"Oh, goody," said Carmen.

"Oh, no," said Fox.

24

"Now, single file,"

said Miss Moon.

"Fire drills are wild!"

said Carmen.

The class got out of the building
in a hurry.

Dexter sat on a piece
of waxed paper
to make himself go even faster.

"Whee!" said Carmen.

"You're next, Fox,"
said Miss Moon.

Fox looked down.

"I don't care for this," he said.

"Go on, Fox," said Miss Moon.

But Fox didn't move.

"Come on, Fox!" said the others.

"It's fun!" said Junior.

"It's wild!" said Carmen.

"Fox is scared!" said Dexter.

"You're not afraid, are you?"
said Miss Moon.
"Yes," said Fox.

"There's nothing to be afraid of,"
said Miss Moon.
"It's easy as pie."

"You may go first," said Fox.

"Not on your life!" said Miss Moon.

"*I* always take the stairs."

"You aren't afraid, are you?"
said Fox.

"Uh," said Miss Moon.

"Who is holding up this fire drill?"
said the principal.

"It's Fox," said Dexter.

"Come down this minute,"
said Mr. Sweet.

"And you too, Miss Moon."

"I'll go first," said Fox.

He closed his eyes.

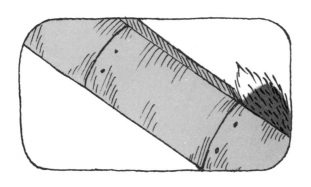

And down he went.

"It's easy as pie!" shouted Fox.

Miss Moon took a deep breath.

And down she went!

The class was very proud of her.

FOX
IN
CHARGE

Carmen, Dexter, and Fox
were on their way to school.
"I'm going to be a pilot
when I grow up," said Carmen.
"I think I'll be a cowboy,"
said Dexter.

"What about you, Fox?"

said Carmen.

"I'm going to be a teacher,"

said Fox.

"You're not serious," said Carmen.

"It's an easy job," said Fox.

That morning

Fox was in for a little surprise.

"I must be away

for a few minutes," said Miss Moon.

"And I am putting Fox in charge."

"Hot dog!" said Fox.

"Keep them under control,"

said Miss Moon.

"Don't worry about a thing,"

said Fox.

"You will mind Fox,"

said Miss Moon to the class.

"Yes, Miss Moon," said the class.

"I'll be back,"

said Miss Moon.

And she left the room.

"Open your readers, please,"
said Fox.

"You can't make us,"
said the class.

"I'm in charge here," said Fox.

"You will do as I say."

"That's what *you* think!"

said the class.

"We're going to have some fun!"

And in no time at all

the room was a real zoo.

Junior threw spitballs.

Dexter stuck gum on Betty's tail.

And Carmen showed everyone

her underpants.

The class was out of control.

Fox looked out into the hall.

"Here she comes!"

he cried.

Everyone sat down—fast.

They sat and waited for Miss Moon.

She did not come.

"You tricked us!" said Dexter.

"Now we're *really* going

to go hog-wild!"

And they did.

All of a sudden

the principal stepped into the room.

He was hopping mad!

"What is the meaning of this?"
said Mr. Sweet.

"It's all Fox's fault!" said Dexter.

"He's in charge."

"Is that so, Dexter?" said Mr. Sweet.

"He couldn't keep us under control,"
said Dexter.
"I think someone should come
with me to the office,"
said Mr. Sweet.

"Uh-oh," said Fox.

When Miss Moon came back,
she found the class all quiet.
"How nice," she said.

"But where is Dexter?"
"He's in the principal's office,"
said the class.